DUNGEONS & DRAGONS

DAME BEATRICE J. DELACROIX III's
— GUIDE FOR TRAINING —
YOUR NEW BEHOLDER

T0364036

Hachette Book Group supports the right to free expression and the value of copyright. The purpose of copyright is to encourage writers and artists to produce the creative works that enrich our culture.

The scanning, uploading, and distribution of this book without permission is a theft of the author's intellectual property. If you would like permission to use material from the book (other than for review purposes), please contact permissions@hbgusa.com. Thank you for your support of the author's rights.

RP Minis®
Hachette Book Group
1290 Avenue of the Americas, New York, NY 10104
www.runningpress.com
@Running_Press

First Edition: April 2022

Published by RP Minis, an imprint of Perseus Books, LLC, a subsidiary of Hachette Book Group, Inc. The RP Minis name and logo is a registered trademark of the Hachette Book Group.

The Hachette Speakers Bureau provides a wide range of authors for speaking events. To find out more, go to www.hachettespeakersbureau.com or call (866) 376-6591.

The publisher is not responsible for websites (or their content) that are not owned by the publisher.

ISBN: 978-0-7624-7886-6

CONGRATULATIONS ON YOUR PURCHASE of a slightly used Beholder from Dame Beatrice J. Delacroix III's Menagerie of Unusual Kind. Our Beholders are known throughout the city for their cutting intelligence, toned eye stalks, and otherworldly charm. This guide will walk you through the first days of Beholder ownership, and by its final pages you'll be as knowledgeable as any Beholder owner this side of the Far Realm. (Per company policy, all sales are final. No refunds. **Absolutely** no returns.)

—BJD III

So, you got yourself a Beholder.

You might be feelin' some regret right now? A good punch in the gut of "What in the seven blazes was I thinking?" But don't you worry. Name's Pip Delacroix, granddaughter of Dame Beatrice J. Delacroix III, and I'm here to settle your nerves with this guide. It might help knowin' regretful feelings are a regular condition among our customers. By the end of this guide, you'll be feeling many things, but I promise you—sealed with a drop o' my own blood and all—regret'll be the last thing on your mind.

Caring for Your Beholder

I'd love to tell you the first day caring for your Beholder'll be the most challenging, but I ain't a liar. So, take a deep breath, a swig o' the good stuff, and load the Beholder into a wagon for your return journey. (You brought one of those, right?) The Menagerie recommends movin' quiet-like through the city and sticking to alleys. The darker the better. City guard don't take to kind to Beholders, even when they're dazed halfway to the Far Realm.

Once home, give your Beholder a quick examination while it's still under the effects of Dame Beatrice J. Delacroix III's Tranquilization Serum. This'll give you a chance to examine your Beholder's body in safety, making sure all the eye stalks are in place and such. Some things to look out for:

- Beware the stare! Fools who stumble on un-tranquilized Beholders often remark upon the malevolence of the beast's great bulging eye and eye

stalks. 'Course, it's also usually the
last thing they say, and we all know
the gravity of life's final words.

- If the eyes ain't enough, Beholders
  also got a set (or two, not sure
  myself . . .) of biters sharp enough to
  make a dragon jealous. We recommend
  using Dame Beatrice J. Delacroix III's
  Dental Paste and Brush for quality
  care of your Beholder's maw.

- You and me, we've got to use clumsy
  hands and feet to get things done,
  but Beholders can do all sorts of fun

things with levitation and magic. You ain't lived until you've seen a Beholder poach an egg.

Got it? Now, rest up. Memorize some spells. Fetch the breastplate stretcher. Stock up on supplies. Get prepared. You're gonna need it.

'Round lunchtime, you might notice Dame Beatrice J. Delacroix III's Tranquilization Serum ain't working quite as well as when you picked up your Beholder. Here's a couple things to remember:

- Dame Beatrice J. Delacroix III's Menagerie of Unusual Kind **does not** offer refunds or returns on products.
- Beholders are naturally independent, so you want to give yours the impression you're unreservedly subservient.

Darien Twelvefingers once said to his cabal, "Through subservience, dominance," and most o' those who didn't listen ended up floatin' face down in Chionthar River with a crimson smile. Good advice.

Setting up your new Beholder's domain

You ever woke up in a daze after a thirsty night and a few too many bar fights? Much more pleasant to wake up in bed next to your kin than a cold jail cell, yeah? Ain't no different for your Beholder. Make 'em a home they want to come back to, and you'll have a happy Beholder. Mostly.

Consider a spacious, enclosed area. For those keen on keepin' their skin, pile on some layers of protection during the move. For your convenience, The Menagerie carries a line of one-size-fits-all protective clothing with arcane wards woven into the fabric by our finest wizards.[*]

City dwellers might think o' an abandoned warehouse down by the docks, or maybe up in the aromatic tanning district. Top it off with cosmetic niceties to make it feel cozy. Stalactites, tepid pools of water, dungeon cells. It's the little things, right? Rural

---

[*] The Menagerie's clothing and protective wear is non-refundable, non-returnable, and non-guaranteed.

folk can save time by findin' a mountain cave or an abandoned den.

Beholders make for ferocious companions should trouble find you while clearing out a new home. Just set it loose on the problematic squatters, dock workers, or bugbear, turn your back for a spell, and all your problems'll disappear. Nearby youngsters should cover their eyes and plug their ears, lest they suffer, let's call it . . . "avoidable trauma."

Word o' warning, Beholders got a tendency to collect devout followings of unsavory types. Some might call 'em cult-like, but we like to think of 'em as fervently lost fellows seeking answers to life's hardest questions. For this reason, we suggest reducing your Beholder's contact with other humans until it feels sufficiently loyal to its new owner: you.

Taming your Beholder

Maybe you broke a horse once or house-trained a hound? Spoke firm, threw 'em a bone for bein' on their best behavior? Forged a bond of mutual respect? Great.

Don't do any o' that with your Beholder.

By my reckoning—and I reckon a lot—Beholders are some o' the most domineering products we handle at The Menagerie. I always tell new owners to establish an appropriate hierarchy of command upon

acquaintance. Right quick—or you'll
lose your chance, then your life. Just
like Beholders ain't got hooves and
definitely don't go drooling all over
your new rug, you gotta treat 'em a
little different. Bow your head a little
bit. Lie prostrate on the floor. Let
'em know who's boss.

Beholders can be exquisitely violent. If you're still reading this, it's not too late to invest in The Menagerie's line of protective wearables. If this does not fit your budget, we recommend a spell of greater invisibility. Can never be too careful, and a Beholder cannot dominate what it cannot see.*

—BJD III

---

* Not guaranteed.

Adventure, Your Beholder, and You

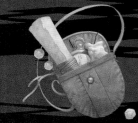

So, you're wonderin' how your new Beholder might fit with the three pillars of adventure? I got advice here that'll leave your friends right speechless.

EXPLORATION

Establishing territory over their new domain is very important for Beholders, and they'll be unfavorable to the idea of leavin' any time soon. Instead, they like having a bunch o' subordinates at their beck and call. Little rats scurrying underfoot. Don't go offering up anyone you care about—but perhaps a great uncle or troublesome employee who needs a dose of . . . let's call it "perspective."

In the event you *do* need to take your Beholder out of the house, be gentle in suggestin' a destination, and prepare to be diverted from your goals when their domineering personality overshadows whatever you had planned.

SOCIAL INTERACTION

The Menagerie recommends against social interaction for Beholder owners. Sure, you want to impress your friends (we all do), but many of our customers report displeasure at the immediate results of socializing their Beholders. Common complaints include loss of friends, limb, and life.

If you must, maybe meet up with some grudging rivals, an unscrupulous politician or that bully who pulled down your pants when you were a kid. He's got it coming to 'im.

COMBAT

So, you wanna bring a knife to a fist fight? Well, what you've got in your possession is more like a sword. A really, really big sword. The trick here is to point it in the direction of your enemies, and let it go wild. Just . . .

don't get in its way before it's done,
and *definitely* don't let it notice you
when there are no more miscreants
to fight. Better yet, just let it loose
and slink away. If you've done your
job setting up its secret lair, your
Beholder should make its way home
on its own.

Whatever you do, don't go looking
for it.

–DAY FIVE–
UNCHARTED TERRITORY

You're . . . still alive. By the seven bloody blazes, can't say I was expectin' this. Oh, dear.

I'm gonna be straight with you, valued customer. Nobody makes it past day four. You're an . . . anomaly. A variable we ain't had to add up before.

So, what's next? When my plans are a shambles, I always turn to ol' Gramma Delacroix for advice. And what does she always say to me? "Ain't no shame in runnin' from your problems," she says. "Now rub my feet, girlie. They sore from runnin'."

Just remember: **no refunds or returns**.

Congratulations! This marks your successful graduation from Dame Beatrice J. Delacroix III's Menagerie of Unusual Kind's training program.

—BJD III

This book has been bound using
handcraft methods and Smyth-sewn
to ensure durability.

The box and interior were designed
by Rachel Peckman.

The text was written
by Aidan Moher.